BILLIONAIRE'S FERTILE RISK

Dark Hucow BDSM

Leandra Camilli

ISBN: 9798848557770
Imprint: Independently published

1st edition

Cover design by: Leandra Camilli

CONTENTS

Title Page

Copyright

Chapter 1 1

Chapter 2 5

Chapter 3 9

Chapter 4 13

Chapter 5 17

Epilogue 21

Teaser: He Owns Me 23

Similar Books 27

About the Author 29

CHAPTER 1

I crossed my legs in an attempt to make myself feel less desperate about my current situation. I looked back at everything that happened so far and the only thing I could think about was how much despair blazed my heart at the moment. The truth was that I was unemployed, didn't have the degree I wanted, and I also kept on thinking back about my family and how much they ruined my life.

But nothing of that mattered right now. An ad had just popped up on the screen, showing something that caught my attention in an instant.

If you are unemployed and looking for something different from work, then this might be the chance you are looking for!

I scrolled down, finding out that the ad mentioned something about turning my body into a business. I didn't know what that was about, but my interest was piqued. So, I kept on scrolling until I found the button to go to the website.

When I was on it, my eyes widened at what the screen was showing me. Without a shred of thought, it was not safe for work. Thinking that, I chuckled.

Naked women with big, oversized breasts. Milk leaking from the nipples... I couldn't help but feel dazed by the sight.

Why would something like that even cross my mind when I was unemployed and didn't have to be looking over my shoulder all the time? It wasn't like when I was still living with my family.

The only way I was making some money now – enough to pay the rent – was thanks to a career that I started online. My 'career' in producing short, intense videos of me naked wasn't going anywhere, really…

Either way, what I thought about all that didn't matter right now. What mattered was that the ad's description was enticing. I didn't want to think this could be the chance I was looking for to get out of this shithole, but it… could really be.

After clicking on the submission form, I realized how easy this would be. Just send some information to them about me and what I thought I was going to get out of this after they accepted me.

What else did the page say? I asked myself, scrolling down on the website for a little while longer until I got the answer to my question.

If you are looking to become a hucow, this might be the chance for you. What you are going to be doing is pretty simple. You won't be working for us, but we will be working for you. We'll take all the milk you can make, sell it, and you will get 40% of the generated revenue. Some of our hardest workers are making around 100k per year doing almost absolutely nothing.

It really is a no-brainer.

100k per year? It wasn't a lot, but it was still tempting. For someone that depended on the money that my clients sent me as donations, it was more than enough to force me to make up my mind about this.

So, I didn't waste any time, filling out the form and then clicking on send. My heart was tight.

It was like that thanks to the information my eyes read when I was browsing the website. It mentioned something about selling me to the 'right' person. Someone that valued me so much that he thought I was worth the purchase…

Of course, this was all consensual. It couldn't be any different.

I wouldn't be doing this if I felt I was being forced to do so. I signed the submission form, sent it to them, and just couldn't stop thinking about how exciting it would be when I was living under the roof of the person that decided to acquire me.

Although, I wasn't going to lie about it. The fact that someone was going to 'own' me was a little terrifying, but that was only part of the whole thing and how it made me feel about this.

When I became someone's property, he would be able to do everything and anything he wanted to me.

Not to mention that becoming a hucow… was tempting.

Well, it was also going to resolve a certain issue with my body that was nagging me these last few months. Someone that I hated a lot had told me that she couldn't believe that I was still so skinny even though I always ate everything and anything I wanted.

She just didn't know anything about me. Sighing, I stood up and then proceeded to the bathroom. Even though it was the dead of the night, I felt like checking myself out in the mirror to make sure that I looked right for the person that would later acquire me. Still, I supposed that I was putting too much hope into this.

There was a very good chance that I could end up falling into the hands of a monster, someone that would make my life a living hell.

And yet, there was no point in worrying about that right now. I had hit rock bottom, after all. After trying everything, including coding and being a programmer, nothing of that was for me anymore.

Nothing wrong with my hair.

Nothing wrong with my face.

Nothing wrong with my body.

I looked just fine, really. At least, that was what I was thinking when I realized that the screen of my phone was showing a notification. I rushed over to it in a heartbeat and I picked it up, holding it in my trembling hands.

The notification was from the hucow website, and I couldn't be more excited about what it meant. Finally, this was the turnaround that my life needed. I could imagine myself becoming someone's plaything.

It looked like that was what was going to happen, too. After I rechecked some things in my profile, I realized that someone was already interested in acquiring me. However, he also mentioned that he wanted to see me in person tonight.

That was, only if I was interested in going on with this.

I could, of course, always go back on my decision, after all.

CHAPTER 2

I was here sitting on the couch and waiting for my master. He said that he was going to come soon, but it had already been minutes since then. I was growing impatient. I didn't want to be waiting anymore for him, especially given that he asked me to be naked.

I mean, he didn't ask me to be naked himself. Actually, it was someone else that told me to do that. His butler or someone like that. He was just an old, geriatric man, and I really couldn't care less about him. I didn't even know why I was thinking about him at the moment.

Even though I didn't see my master yet, his portrait was hanging on the wall above the fireplace. And... Wow. He was just stunning. The man was smoking hot, which only made me think how fortunate I was that he was the one that acquired me.

Still, I was horny, especially now that I was also feeling slightly sleepy and not much was happening in here. It was so silent here in the living room and all throughout his house that my heart was tight, with my mind thinking, all the time, that something or someone was going to jump out of the shadows to hurt me.

Not to mention that my being sleepy also meant that I was also horny, especially with that portrait hanging above the fireplace. I knew that it would not be appropriate to think of myself when I was where everybody could see me, but it wasn't like my mind could understand something like that.

In fact, it was doing everything in its power to make me lower my hand and search for my pussy.

I turned my head left and right, hoping that I was going to convince myself that I should really not do this. I just knew what would then happen. One of the butlers or the maids would find me doing that, proceeding to tell Mr. Lawrence about it.

Gosh, I just never felt so out of place and so much in the right place at the same time, considering that one of my obsessions was fingering myself where everybody could see me. I only never did that because I didn't want to be locked up for public masturbation.

Well, no time to be thinking about that. I already made a decision and there was no going back anymore. So, without giving it a second thought, I started to nudge my clit, pressing my finger on it in different directions slowly and carefully.

I was only doing this so that my mind could stop nagging me about it. Really, that was everything that was happening, but there was also no denying that it was turning me on so much.

Finally, I was realizing one of my dreams. Public masturbation.

Gosh, my mind was so fucked up.

But then again, my finger was so nice, moving left and right, enjoying my clit. I could even feel some wetness seeping out of the folds, which was only making this a bigger turn-on than it already was.

Not to mention that my body was beginning to get hotter, I could feel my breathing quickening, and sweat was beginning to come out of the pores in my skin.

Truly, everything was happening so that I orgasmed right in here, in the living room, and I couldn't do anything about that. Not anymore, anyway. It was too late. My finger was moving faster against my clit, my breathing accelerating, more sweat covering my skin, and that rising sensation building up in my body was the cherry on top.

It was too much.

But just when I thought it was really going to happen, a voice shot through the air. "Stop what you are doing. I didn't allow you to do that, princess."

I snapped my head to the right, where the voice was coming from. That was him. Mr. Lawrence, in all his glory, but he didn't come here the way I thought he was going to. He was actually still dressed, which was disappointing.

I thought he would come into the living room naked and ready to eat me raw.

I stopped moving my finger on my clit, my pre-orgasm fading away.

"I'm sorry, Master. I was only enjoying myself because I couldn't stop looking at your portrait above the fireplace without thinking about how big your cock is and wondering what it would be like when you were fucking me."

"Me fucking you? Do you really think that it's going to happen so easily? You do realize that I have many women living with me that would kill for an opportunity to do that, right?"

I opened my mouth but shut it right away. He had other women with him other than his wife? I couldn't believe it. The ad and the website hadn't said anything about that.

But now, analyzing his face a little more, I could tell that he had just told me the truth. He was looking at me with such a serious stare. I felt as if it was penetrating right into my soul.

"I'm really sorry, Master. It will never happen again, I promise."

And even though that was what I said, I had no idea if I would be able to follow through with it.

"I don't believe you."

When he said that, I felt my heart jumping in my chest. Was the punishment going to start so early on? I didn't know, but the way that he was still analyzing me with his piercing eyes made me feel that it was part of his plans. "There's something we can do to start this the right way. It's something that I was actually planning on doing even before coming here."

I didn't know what that was, but my interest was certainly piqued right now.

CHAPTER 3

"What is that, Master?" I asked when he started to step toward me. Uh-oh. He was going to punish me. Without a shred of doubt, that was what he was going to do, splaying me on his lap and then pounding his hand on my ass over and over again, showing me how disappointed he was by my acts after coming here.

Mr. Lawrence stood before me, his hands going to his belt. He undid it, letting it fall to the floor. Then, he lowered his pants and his underwear, his dick springing out and looking threatening.

I gasped. Something as big as that shouldn't even exist and yet here he was showing it to me without displaying as much as a sliver of shame. He wrapped his fingers around it, stroking the skin gently.

And in the meantime, it was like my eyes were mesmerized by the sight. I found myself incapable of blinking, imagining that thick, oversized prick thrusting into my mouth.

Gosh, was all of this really happening or was I only imagining it?

"Suck it, bitch, and do it slowly and nicely. I want to see how long you can make me last," he threatened, his voice echoing in the silence in the living room.

I couldn't help but check the sides, making sure that nobody was coming in here that could destroy the mood that was already settling between us. I mean, I didn't want to shock anyone seeing me with my lips wrapped around his gland.

His cock was nice, thick, and pre-come was oozing from the tip. To say that the sight was pushing all the right buttons in me would be an understatement.

Well, Mr. Lawrence gave me the go-ahead, so there was no point in delaying the inevitable. Without giving it a second thought, I just wrapped my lips around the gland, wondering if he was going to notice that this was the first time I was doing this.

I was getting into a nice rhythm when he grabbed a handful of my hair, thrusting my head all the way down. What the fuck! I barely had enough time to process what was happening. In a blur, I could already feel my nose pressing against the skin of his crotch and the tip of his cock pounding onto the back of my throat, making me gag and cough.

And yet, it wasn't enough.

I was focused on what I was doing when I noticed someone behind Mr. Lawrence. It was a woman wearing a dark red dress, and even though I was not a lesbian, I could tell that she was eye-catching. She wasn't like me, either. There was an aura around her that told me she was someone special to Mr. Lawrence.

And yet, whoever she was, didn't matter right now. I was making such a mess, gobbling up his dick like it was nothing. Seconds after he thrust it into my mouth and down my throat, I wasn't going to deny that it was difficult, but now my tongue and lips were worshiping everything.

Saliva continued to smear the entirety of his prick, little moans escaping my hungry mouth.

And even everything that was happening wasn't enough. I wanted more. I started to play with his balls, which were heavy with his milk. They hung low, making this even better. I could move them between my fingers, my digitals dancing on them.

"Fuck, fuck," Mr. Lawrence moaned, his dick erupting all of a sudden in my mouth. Shooting rope after rope of his come, I was jubilant and feeling so much more than I thought I would be feeling when he was dumping his load in me.

I felt it scorching the skin of my throat. That was how hot it was.

And it was shaking inside my mouth like it was a trapped beast. I had to hold it with both of my hands so that it would not slip out. It was difficult, but I managed to keep his dick jammed in my throat, squirting out the last lines of his thick, sticky release.

When he was done, I even gave his scrotum a couple of licks. That was how much I worshiped it. I even looked up, searching for his eyes. Even though he was still staring seriously at me, there was no denying that he enjoyed how I worked his prick.

"That was good. I'm not going to punish you anymore right now. I think that you deserve that at least for showing that you can give head," he explained and I couldn't feel more jubilant about this than I already was.

"Thank you, Master. I'm really so happy that you enjoyed it," I said and he pulled his pants and underwear back on, which was disappointing. My mind went back to the woman wearing that dark red dress and why she was in the doorway, watching us from afar.

Who was she? I was certain that she wasn't Mrs. Lawrence because, just like the website said, she was locked up in the basement.

"What are you going to do now, Master?" I asked.

"I'm going to my bedroom and lie down. I need to sleep. Tomorrow, we will have a full day together. I approve of you living here, so I want to make sure that your transformation will happen smoothly and that you will become one of our most productive hucows."

My heart sped up, thinking about that. So, my Master finally accepted me. He decided to acquire me definitively and now there was no turning back anymore.

I watched him as he went up the stairs, my eyes scrutinizing every part of his body. He was just so tall, so imposing, and his backside was thick, wide, and... Wow. I could imagine myself sliding my hands across that for hours on end while he pounded in and out of me.

CHAPTER 4

It was quite difficult not to be thinking about Mr. Lawrence when he was disappointing me so much. He said that he was going to come here and milk me for the first time now that my transformation was over, and yet he was nowhere to be seen.

I was in the basement with the woman that wore that eye-catching, dark red dress.

"I've seen you here before and I just can't help but wonder who you are."

"Oh, silly. You don't really need to worry about me. I'm here just to study this new business venture that Geoffrey is starting, that's all."

When she said that, I couldn't help but wonder if she was bullshitting me. It wouldn't be the first time someone here was doing that, after all.

But she was indeed holding a notepad and a pen. She circled me, taking notes, analyzing every part of my body with her attentive eyes. I did feel a little uncomfortable and shy with her walking around me and saying nothing while she took notes, but I still couldn't say no.

"Mr. Lawrence... Wow, I can't stop thinking about him. When do you think he's going to come?" I asked when she stopped.

She put the notepad and the pen inside her shoulder bag, closing it.

"I really don't know. I'm just happy that he is letting me stay here for a little while so that I understand better how all of this happens."

I sighed, flicking my finger on my clit and rubbing it. I closed my eyes and fantasized about Mr. Lawrence pounding in and out of me, fucking me into oblivion - and also doing the one thing that he should do, which was to take my virginity and impregnate me with his heir.

It would never happen. At least, that was what I was telling myself so that I didn't start to dream too high.

"You really know that you shouldn't do that. You know that Geoffrey doesn't like it when his subjects start to please themselves without his command."

Speaking was difficult, but I still had to reply, "I just can't stop myself. I want to feel his big dick pounding into my fertile, virgin pussy. I want to feel him coming inside of me, shooting his potent, sticky seed in my womb and keeping it there until I'm finally carrying his heir in me."

She chuckled, taking her shoulder bag. "Funny that you all feel the same way about him. I really don't know much about Geoffrey, but I'm just so happy that he's here doing his manly duty, taking your virginities."

And just when she said that, he started to descend the steps of the stairs. He stood imperious. This time, he decided to impress me by coming here without his clothes on. He was naked from top to bottom and even though it was dark here in the basement, there was enough light to distinguish his muscles and how they changed and curved. I couldn't help but feel my mouth watering at the thought of sliding my hand over his abs.

It was breathtaking.

And yet, I knew that I made a mistake and that this time he wasn't going to let it slide. I could see that in the way that he slightly squinted his eyes. He was disappointed and a little mad at what his eyes were witnessing.

"What did I tell you about pleasuring yourself when I'm not around? I'm the only one that is allowed to please you, Ashley."

"I'm really sorry, Master. Please punish me. I just couldn't contain my hunger and lust anymore."

"Oh, I'm going to do so much more than just punish you," he threatened, approaching me.

"And I think that I'm going to make myself scarce," the woman in the red dress slipped out of the basement, moving so fast she was like a blur. I barely had enough time to register that she wasn't here anymore with us when I noticed that Mr. Lawrence was already right in front of me.

A single bench stood by the wall closest to us. He dropped his butt on it, spreading me on his lap.

I didn't know if he knew anything about this, but I enjoyed that I could feel his manhood pressing against my pussy. It was already hard. That was how I knew that most of this was just him pretending that he was pissed by me pleasuring myself.

He didn't really actually care about that as much as he cared about punishing me with his rough, dominating right hand.

"30 slaps for that infraction," he promised. I felt his voice reverberating in the basement. It was so big that I couldn't see his wife and the other hucows. I knew that they were somewhere in here, but it was too dark and my eyes could not catch sight of them.

"Yes, Daddy," I said, breathless and gritting my teeth. It was going to be so good.

"Don't 'yes, daddy' me," he grumbled, striking my butt one, two, three times and then all the subsequent times after that, making me gasp and feel the pain waving through my body.

I felt my skin stinging, sweat pouring out on my forehead.

When it was over, I noticed that his dong was even harder than before. I wondered if he was thinking about taking my virginity right now. After all, the punishment was over. I knew that if he found me pleasuring myself again, he would punish me even harder than just now, but I wasn't worried about that.

What I was thinking about was how long his dick was. Like, 10 inches? Maybe 11? I didn't know, but it made my mouth water so much I just couldn't stop thinking about it.

Then, I slid off his lap, falling on the floor in the basement.

I looked up and found his rod, and I knew that finally, he was going to do the one thing that he should. Not to mention that my jugs were filled with milk, so he could finally milk me for the first time, too.

I wondered if he was going to use the milking machine or his own lips for that.

Well, I supposed that it didn't matter the way that he did it as long as he did it.

CHAPTER 5

"Come here, you little brat," he shouted, taking me in his arms and then pulling me up and making me sit on his lap again. This time, his cock was pressing up against my cunt again, and I felt the waves of pleasure that this was generating in me.

"I'm so sorry, Master, for being so bratty and naughty."

His eyes studied me, his lips parting slightly.

"Don't worry about it." He took a deep breath, smelling me. "You smell so nice. I can feel the smell of your milk in the air. I want everything."

And after he said that, he took one of my melons in his hand, guiding the nipple into his mouth. I gasped. I didn't think that he was going to be so direct when doing that.

His fingers were rough and they pressed into my skin, pushing out as much milk as he could. He gave my boob little squeezes and each of them shot rope after rope of my milk in his mouth.

Master closed his eyes, humming as he chugged down all of my milk. It was all happening so quickly that, in a moment, I realized that my breast was already getting empty.

He was far from being done with that breast, too, even after I noticed some of the milk escaping his mouth through the sides. It wasn't just his hand that was squeezing my breast slightly, but also the pressure that his lips were applying on the bottom of my nipple.

What he was doing was generating so much pleasure in me that I started to rub my pussy on his dick, making it even harder. He was so big and thick that I could not help but wonder how much pleasure and pain he would make me feel when he finally breached me.

"Oh God, oh God," I said over and over, breathless. I could feel that rising sensation of my climax building up in me and I knew that, when it finally burst, it would wash over my entire body.

And yet, Master had no intention of stopping what he was doing. He just kept on drinking and consuming all of my milk until he couldn't anymore. My cunt was leaking with my pleasure.

A moment later, he finally pulled his head back, his eyes gazing at me and taking in the sight of my face in front of him.

Milk lines descended on his face, going down to his neck.

He wiped his mouth with his hand, licking the fingers clean. "It's so delicious. I can tell that you are going to be one of the most productive hucows in here."

And I was going to be making 100k per year, too. I couldn't be more overjoyed, remembering that.

"I'm so happy with that, Master."

He purred, saying, "and I'm far from done with you right now, Ashley."

He took my other nipple into his mouth, doing everything he did before, but this time to my other breast. He emptied it, making me moan and come again, my pussy vibrating on his cock.

In the meantime, I was wondering when he would finally take my virginity.

Master pulled his head back one more time, this time suggesting that he was going to make me do something even more filthy than before. My mind was racing, thinking about that.

"Lie down on the floor, lift your ass up, and keep it pointed at me. I think that it's finally time to take your V card, don't you agree?" He asked me and I nodded. I showed my excitement by lying down on the floor and raising my ass, doing everything exactly the way he wanted it.

"You can fuck me now, master," I said and he smiled, positioning himself right behind me. His fingers pressed and massaged my butt as if he was assessing what was new territory to him. After all, it was the first time that he was going to fuck me, and he wanted to do it right.

He nudged his prick onto the entrance of my pussy, his fingers still feeling and loving my asscheeks.

"I'm going to do so much more than that," he said before jamming his rod into my tunnel, doing so without showing any shred of mercy for me. He went all the way in like a speeding train, punching through my hymen. I gasped, feeling waves of pain shooting through my body.

My vision darkened and I thought I was going to pass out, but I didn't.

His pace, in the beginning, was fast but controlled, and he knew exactly what he was doing. He was so deep in me that I could feel him striking his balls against my ass, and it was a feeling that I would never forget.

Sweat glimmered on my body and breathing was becoming so much harder than it usually was.

As he continued to piston in and out of me, he brought me over the edge and I came in record time.

"I'm so sorry I came so fast, Master," I confessed, whimpering.

He slid his hand across the nape of my neck, massaging it.

"Don't worry about that, little Princess. There's so much more that you can do to make up for it," he murmured behind me, bending his body on top of mine and then continuing to pound in and out of me, fucking me into oblivion.

Then, Mr. Lawrence erupted, filling me to the brim with his milk. I groaned and wailed, never before in my life feeling so much pleasure and pain at the same time. My pussy would never be the same. My ass would never be the same, and it was everything I wanted.

And even after he was done, he still stayed inside of me. I guessed that he just wanted to make sure that not even a single drop of his release would come out...

EPILOGUE

The woman in the dark, red dress was in front of me again, her mouth holding a pen while she read her notes. I wondered what she was thinking right now. She was still so much like a famous beauty model, I thought to myself again.

Still, she was not as wished as I was by Master. She would never be because I doubted that she was even considering the option of becoming a hucow like me.

"So, he really got you pregnant too, didn't he?" She asked me, taking the pen out of her mouth and then holding it in her right hand, turning it left and right. I didn't know why my attention was so focused on it, but I felt my eyes going left and right, following its direction.

"Yeah, he really did."

As I said that, I slid my hands on my big belly, realizing that now it was already months since that morning when he got me pregnant in the basement. I was so overjoyed that I had a life in me now. A part of Master...

"You look so happy about it. I wish that I could be feeling the same way," she said, making me wonder what exactly was going on in her mind right now.

We were with the other hucows, too. They were sitting on a large, long couch positioned across from us on the other side of the room. They were happy, joking, and playing together, more often than not spraying milk all over the floor.

I tsked, seeing that. It was likely that Master would be so pissed off, seeing their erratic behavior, that he would punish them, but right now I wasn't really concerned about what he would do when he finally came from work.

I knew their names. Jenna and Sharon. His wife, Helene, was still locked up in the basement, so we didn't even have to see her often.

Well, she didn't matter right now anyway, so that was something I wasn't even thinking about.

"Well, I'm going out now. I'm happy that you are happy," she said, stepping away from me.

"Bye," I said.

I wasn't the only one that was or had been pregnant. Jenna and Sharon also gave Master some heirs. I couldn't help but wonder what exactly he would do with them when they were older.

My ears picked up the crunching of the asphalt by the tires in front of the house. It was Mr. Lawrence. He had come back from work and now he was going to fuck me again.

This time, it was going to be even milkier and messier than before. He could go all out without thinking about anything, now that I was already pregnant with his heir.

It looked like something in here was changing, too. Someone different coming. Who was she?

The End

Thank you for reading this story. Leave your review. Your feedback helps me immensely!

TEASER: HE OWNS ME

Dark Hucow BDSM (Auction Club - 2)

"Wait, you are not telling me that you are a virgin, right?" My friend asked me. He was with me and I was in his house. We were here having a typical party that happened every time we were together. I had just come here from work. I was traveling abroad and I decided to come here so that we could catch up on some things. There were so many things that were happening in his life, after all.

And one was that he was with a certain auction club. I didn't know what it was about exactly, but he was so jubilant about it when he was talking with me about everything on the phone. He even told me that he was now married, though I couldn't see his wife anywhere.

There were signs in his house that he was already married, but I didn't even see a portrait of them in the house. I wondered what was up with that. But I wasn't really worried about it. What I was concerned about was the fact that he just asked me if I was a virgin or not, and me being me, how was I going to not answer that question, especially when he was being so nice to me, giving me everything?

His eyes were... Intense, to say the least. He had his attention fully focused on me and I didn't know how to react to that. That was why I was feeling so uncomfortable, shifting my weight all the time while I was sitting on the couch.

He chuckled. "Is it really because you are so skinny and your breasts are so small?" He asked me, making my cheeks blush deep red. I never thought that he was going to ask me that question and was going to do it so bluntly.

It was true, I thought, looking down at my body. I tried my best, tried to buy the best clothes possible, but the truth was that not even the best clothes and not even the best treatments – that weren't too invasive – could do much to change my body. I always looked at those photos of those women on the Internet and I always imagined how lucky they were to have such curvy bodies.

But that was all in the past. At least, that was what I was telling myself anyway.

"Yeah, I still am. I really should not be saying anything about that to you right now, though," I said, hoping that he was going to change the subject, but given the way that he was staring at me, it was obvious that he wasn't going to drop it so soon.

"If it bothers you so much, there is something that we could do about it."

"If you are thinking that I'm going to have sex with you, then you are delusional. I'm not going to do that. You are a friend of mine, I think you're hot, but that's where it all ends. I don't want to help you cheat on your wife, who you just recently married."

He sighed, shaking his head. "I was actually thinking about something else. There is this auction club that I go to often, and I think that they are looking for people like you. They say that they have a treatment that is going to change your body forever, and you only have to sign their contract so that they can sell you to someone who might be interested in you. By signing the contract, you will become that person's property and you will have to do everything they want you to do."

I widened my eyes immediately, not believing that I was going to become someone's property. The first thought that popped up into my mind was that I shouldn't do it at all, but then I looked down at my body and I reminded myself how much I hated it, and nothing was going to change that.

"You really don't want to do it?" Marcos asked, winking.

Oh, gosh. The winking. How was I going to say no to something like that? I thought, already feeling some wetness in my pussy. The truth was that the thought of becoming someone's property was tempting. Not to mention the fact that I would be in an auction club, too.

Fuck. Just the thought of all that happening was enough to make me decide on it right away.

"Alright, I guess that this is really happening," I said and he put down the glass that he was holding in his hand. Then, he stood up, his hands taking off his belt. Wait, what the fuck? I asked myself, realizing that this was indeed happening.

"But there's something that you should do for me first. Otherwise, I won't be telling anyone in the auction club about this," he informed, making me drop my jaw. What the fuck was going on with him? Was Marcos really so tempted to cheat on his wife with me? And here I thought that he was happily married to her.

Or maybe he'd always been an asshole and only now was I noticing that. Either way, I didn't like it, even though the thought of sucking him off made me water my mouth.

"Your wife..."

"Forget her. She isn't here. I want you," he said, lowering his pants and showing, for the delight of my eyes, his big, monstrous cock. I couldn't help but look at it and wonder how it was so big.

I also put the glass I was holding back on the coffee table, wrapping my lips around his big, massive, meaty manhood. If this was happening and it really was, then there was no point in pretending that I didn't want it.

So, I went down on his dick, swirling my tongue around it. He put his hand on the back of my head, grabbed a handful of my hair, and then dictated the pace, not letting the fact that this was the first time I was giving head – and thus, was deeply inexperienced – change his thoughts about this. If anything, he was enjoying this a lot more than he should.

Marcos came in my mouth in record time, looking slightly disappointed in himself.

"Sorry. I suppose that I should have held on for a little while longer, but even though you are still a virgin, I can't deny that you are hot and I've always thought about this moment, wondering how I was going to fuck your mouth. It was breathtaking, dear."

And with that said, I knew that my life, from now on, was going to be so different from what it could be.

SIMILAR BOOKS

BUNDLE - HUCOW PRISON

All the books of the Hucow Prison series in one single, convenient collection.

1. Hucow Prison

SERIES - BUMPED HUCOWS

1. Milked by Rockstars

2. Tamed by Rockstars

3. Taken by Rockstars

4. Claimed by Rockstars

SERIES - HIS HERD

1. Peculiar Dairy

2. Milked by her Boyfriend

3. Menage for Milking

4. Farm Milking

5. Fertile for my Farmers

ABOUT THE AUTHOR

Leandra Camilli's obsession? Writing dirty, steamy stories that make her readers drool. She loves her Alpha males, hucows, sissies, and futas. If you're looking for those kinds of books, look no further.

With a cup of coffee on her table and warm socks on, she writes almost every day. Leandra Camilli has featured in several top 100 categories in the store, and she publishes weekly.